Amal Behbehani is a Kuwaiti writer with a master's in business administration and an undergraduate degree in English Language and Literature. For the past five years, she has been an administrative assistant at the Dean of Student Affairs office at the American University of Kuwait. Amal currently resides in Kuwait with her family and a vast collection of Funko Pops, ranting about a fairytale TV show.

To E&N, for your unwavering support in all of my decisions, and
for always believing in me. Love you
Mama and Baba.

Amal Behbehani

DEAR SUITOR

AUSTIN MACAULEY PUBLISHERS™

LONDON • CAMBRIDGE • NEW YORK • SHARJAH

ISBN – 9789948794868 – (Paperback)
ISBN – 9789948794875 – (E-Book)

Application Number: MC-10-01-0482363
Age Classification: 17+

First Published 2023
AUSTIN MACAULEY PUBLISHERS FZE
Sharjah Publishing City
P.O Box [519201]
Sharjah, UAE
www.austinmacauley.ae
+971 655 95 202

A shoutout to the typewriters group, the writing sessions got me to finally get this story written down. Also, the credit goes to my sister, Anwar Behbehani, for her artistic drawing of the cover page.

Dear Diary,

Suitor #3 passed by today. He insisted on having sugar with his tea, practically filling the cup with it. He kept joking about how only 'weak' men couldn't handle all that sugar. After his prideful boast, I motioned to my dad, introducing him, "this is Bo Bader, he has diabetes."

It was very quiet after that.

#

Dear Diary,

My brother wants to die. Specifically, by my hands. He wanted me to meet his friend; kept swearing up and down that he was a good match. Seeing as my brother is only two years younger than me, I assumed his friend would be of the same age. (There is nothing wrong with marrying someone younger; look at Uncle Samer, he is eight years younger than Auntie Fatima.)

So when the old man came in, I assumed he was the father of the expected suitor. When no one else followed him inside, my trickling suspicions were confirmed when I could hear my brother sniggering behind the door.

I sat politely and listened to the man speak of his days in the stock market – Souq al Manakh – both my parents and I smiling through it all. As soon as we escorted him out, which took a while with the old man's walking pace, I turned around and pounced on my brother. It took two of my other brothers to pull me off his laughing traitorous ass.

My cousins kept sending me memes of skeletons dressed up as grooms in the WhatsApp group throughout the day. News travels fast around here.

#

Dear Diary,

Today, the suitor did not even make it through the door. Mama got a call from a woman. Apparently, the woman is in the same WhatsApp group as Mama, and heard that she had two daughters. She kept talking about her son, how he is ready to get married, and how she's heard good things about our family. My mother politely chatted with the woman – she did enjoy socializing with whoever came across her path – and told her that her oldest daughter (aka me), is not currently looking for someone. I was taking a break from seeing people.

The woman was quiet only for a moment, but then continued to say, "What about your other daughter?"

My mom closed the phone after that. "This isn't a *baqala*." She muttered to my dad during lunch.

#

Dear Diary,

Finally, the perfect man showed up! We were into the same shows, the same food, even were interested in traveling to the same places.

Unfortunately, he came to ask for my sister instead.

"It was like sitting with a male version of you." She told me afterwards, once she finished chatting with him. She told him outright no. "I already have one of you, I don't need another copy as well."

… Thanks, I guess?

#

Dear Diary,

Today, Amira (cousin from dad's side, not mom's side), told us about a guy who set his dogs on their house. Thankfully the driver closed the gate on time, but it took a while for the police to arrive. Apparently one of the suitors for her daughter did not find it amusing that she said no. It freaked me out that that could happen to me, and I voiced my concern to my mom. Bader and Salman laughed, saying who would dare to do that with them here? All the guys in the neighborhood knew not to mess with them.

But what if I didn't have any brothers?

#

Dear Diary,

So embarrassing, an epic fail. I was running around work getting ready for an event, and didn't have time to rest before the guy came with his mother. We did the small talk, his mother and my mother trying to figure out if his elder sister's husband is related to us. After moving to the separate living room, I felt the tiredness wash over me but shook it off. He started chatting about his work, his colleagues, and I nodded with each topic. I must have dozed off, because suddenly Mama was nudging my shoulder, her voice laced with concern.

Mama had to keep profusely apologizing to the man's mother as they left. I got a never-ending lecture about how is it I have the ability to stay awake when I'm out with my friends at night, but can barely stay awake for one sitting? Besides feeling annoyed at being lectured, I do feel a bit guilty about falling asleep on the guy.

The next night, my dad hinted at me to drink coffee when we were heading out. Ha, ha.

#

Dear Diary,

I couldn't stop laughing with Salman, so only remembered to write this now.

So, this guy comes to see me. The usual, his mom is friends with my mom, they think we would be a good match, his brother already got married, it's his turn, etc.

So we're sitting there, and his mom and my mom are in the other living room. We go through the usual questions, and then he leans over and goes, "You're kinda hot, you know?"

I could feel my cheeks reddening, and you know, okay, he took me by surprise. But then he started to go over stuff that one doesn't say at the first meet-up. Stuff that happens when you watch HBO shows – after the season finale when the two leads get together. All while his mom is sitting right there in the next room.

So I smiled, told him to text me since I couldn't understand what he's saying (cue Bambi eyes) and he goes and sends me it all in text with a smirk. I smiled back and forwarded his text to his mom and my mom.

Cue the yelling, the guy looking pale as a ghost, and me not seeing other suiters for the next two weeks. I blocked his number as soon as he left. But took a screencap to send to the cousins WhatsApp group and Salman, since he taught me that trick.

"If it's a text he wouldn't send to his mom, he shouldn't be sending to you." Was his one and only advice when I first started seeing suitors.

#

Dear Diary,

It seems useless, to try seeing more suitors. But then I reread the entries, and gotta say, some of them were fun. Maybe one day one of them will click. Maybe.

#

Dear Diary,

This week's suitor came with a list. I'm not kidding, like an actual printed list. He barely said hello before he whipped it out. I thought he brought the marriage contract with him. It turned out to be a check list.

"I just want to make sure we match before going on." The guy says, and starts to go through the list. Do I smoke? Do I drink? What are my working hours at work? Do I travel a lot? Do I want kids? Do I know how to drive?

Do I know how to drive?

Afterwards, my mom explained that he has sat through three engagements before having to break them off when it turns out he and the woman did not want the same things. I felt bad for him, but I also hoped I never reached that level of hopelessness, of turning it into a mechanical system.

Apparently, I matched his list, but he drew the line at me wanting to wait at least a year before we tie the knot. I hope he finds someone, he seemed nice, albeit the list.

#

Dear Diary,

Let us go over which sibling should be at home when the suitor visits.

None of them.

Salman and Bader are so bad. If they're not sniggering from the staircase or throwing random comments, they're giving the suitor the evil eye. I swear to you, their stares even drove one suitor off without even stepping into the house.

I don't think any guy would pass their approval, but hopefully one will survive their teasing.

#

Dear Diary,

Perhaps you're wondering why I'm not writing down the suitor's names. (If a notebook has any consciousness at all – I hope you're at least enjoying my struggles).

That is because: I honestly can't remember all their names. I barely remember people's names when they visit the family, let alone someone who only comes to visit me once. One or two might stand out, but then I feel bad for the rest.

So, diary, the suitors will be anon. You can give them names if you want to. Maybe if THE one shows up, I'll add names, and you can guess – like in *How I Met Your Mother* – who is the winner.

#

Dear Diary,

One word answers don't work. Sure, maybe if we were friends and texting when we're tried. But really? You're getting to know someone, and your answers are all just one word phrases? THEN WHY DID YOU COME TO SEE ME? Just stay at home and text in your answers.

Seriously, I did not pluck my eyebrows and get dressed to talk to a robot. Did he need juice? Sugar? Smoke? Something to jump start his brain? At one point I was close to nudging his shoulder to see if that will start his system.

Even at the end of the meeting, at the door he just said "Okay." Okay? Okay for what? Okay, he came to see me? Okay, he finished the meeting? Okay, the aliens are coming to visit Kuwait?

During lunch, Bader and Dad just answered anything I said with "okay".

#

Dear Diary,

There is one who came with his sister. For a first meeting, I suppose that's not weird. It could be a great icebreaker, maybe he wanted me to feel comfortable to talk with him. He is five years older than me, and his sister is around the same age as me. They both sat across from me, and the sister and I started to chat. And continued chatting. By the end of the visit, I doubt I said a word to the suitor, though I did get to exchange with his sister our Tumblr accounts.

I'm still in touch with his sister, she has a really good collection of TV show recommendations. From her I found out he eventually got married.

#

Dear Diary,

Today's suitor was bad. Like, really bad. I don't want to mention him. The only good thing about today is Bader and Salman let me choose the movie for tonight, and didn't tease me about it.

#

Dear Diary,

The suitor with the list came back to negotiate. It seems I ticked off most of what he has jotted down, compared to other candidates. Because it's the first time someone has come for a second meeting, my mom insisted I give him a second chance. I did not have any high expectations at all, but I was intrigued.

He came on time, and I made small talk with his mother for a few minutes before we moved to a separate couch. He doesn't take out the list this time, but directly asks me if I'll agree to tying the knot in less than a year. He wanted to start a family as soon as possible.

I've heard from relatives and friends about a quick engagement. About it not being enough time to get to know the other person. But on the other hand, even a year of meetings won't be enough to truly know how a person is in private. Perhaps the Americans with living together and dating for years have the upper hand in having time to get to know the person. But I had to base it purely on the man's family name and the impression I get of him. But also, you hear a lot of stories about suddenly finding their spouse in an affair, or not the person they're pretending to be. So does anyone really know who they get in bed with?

Still, those thoughts were swirling in my head while I had to answer his question. In all honesty, I wasn't ready to settle down. Call me crazy, but I wanted to be wooed first. Or at least, not get married within the same year of meeting the guy. I tried to explain, but I don't think he understood my reasons in delaying. He was polite the rest of the evening, but hasn't called after to confirm if this is something to continue.

#

Dear Diary,

Today I joked at a family gathering that if I didn't get engaged by the age of thirty, I'll marry the first guy who walks by.

The aunties did not take it well, and lectured me about giving myself more credit than marrying any random bloke. I'm honestly touched they expected more for me, and didn't mind that I'm so late in the game.

#

Dear Diary,

… This is the first time in these arranged meetings that the guy just sits there in silence. Just a hello, and then the next twenty minutes, not one single word. At first I waited for him to say something – they usually have questions and honestly sometimes I feel overwhelmed to be the one starting a conversation with a guy I don't know – but as five, then ten minutes pass with us just sitting there, I asked how his day was. He shrugged. I asked how his family was. He nodded. I asked if he had a favorite show, and he shrugged again.

He was dressed in the traditional *disdasha* and *gitra*, all buttons buttoned and cloth ironed and pressed. It did seem he put in a lot of effort to look nice for this meeting. But didn't try to interact at all. I just shrugged to my mom when she glanced our way.

At the end his mom thanked us for letting them in, and they went their way.

#

Dear Diary,

I'm a 90s kid, I'm not ashamed to say that. Probably spent most of my childhood watching all the movies that came out in that decade. And one of those movies that I still remember vividly, is *It Takes Two* with the Olsen twins. And one specific quote that stuck with me to this day.

That can't eat, can't sleep, reach for the stars over the fence, world series kind of love.

I guess I am waiting for that kind of love, and I can't find it in any of these meetings.

#

Dear Diary,

I really don't like it when someone parks in my place, especially when it's our house! My parents are lenient with the neighbors, but this time they took it too far. I had to park in the sun and walk over with the boxes I had to take back from work. Our driver would place a nice note on the neighbor's car to move it, but this time I scrawled on the paper and pushed it inside the barely opened window.

Striding into home, I started calling out for Mom, "Seriously, mama, talk to the neighbors, *mayseer* they use our parking sp—"

I freeze in the middle of the living room. My mom's smile tells me I'm in trouble, as she reminds me that today her cousin's friend was coming to see me.

"Ah, yes, sorry about that," I laughed and quickly texted my brother to get the driver to remove the sign from the prospective car.

Of course Salman was asleep and didn't see the message. Of course the mother left my mom a very interesting text about that. Thank god I didn't slash their tires (as if I ever would, but still, the thought counts).

#

Dear Diary,

He looks familiar. He looks famous. He looks fancy. I just couldn't put my finger on where I've seen him. The nanny is practically hyperventilating by the door. I didn't get to ask my mom for the boy's name before we were sitting across from each other. I was late coming in from a breakfast outing, and didn't read the family WhatsApp group chat. But I promised my dad I'll try these "blind" meetings, and so I smile and answer his questions. He blinks in surprise when I ask what he does, and smiles when I ask if I've seen him play when he mentions soccer. Salman keeps messaging me, and I apologize to the guy as I silence my phone. We chatted for a while, but there was no chemistry at all, barely even interest as the meeting dragged on. He thanked me for accepting the meeting, and left.

It's only later when I check my phone do I see Salman asking for his autograph. Apparently he's on the national soccer team.

#

Dear Diary,

While we waited for the next guy to come visit, my mother asked me if I wanted to stop these meetings. It's the first time she brings it up. I think the polite or modest answer would be to say yes, just stop these meetings, I'm meeting too many guys. But other than these meetings, I don't see how I'll meet someone the proper way. So I tell her no, lets continue till the right one shows up.

20

I doubt either of us thought that would happen in the upcoming meeting though.

#

Dear Diary,

Yesterday the guy was a no show. My mom called his aunt, who explained he changed his mind. Since I was already dressed up, and my parents in one of the rare good moods where we can suggest new ideas, we told them lets go to brunch. Bader was out with his friends, but Salman came and met with us at the café. It was nice being out with the family.

#

Dear Diary,

Penelope had nothing on my batch of suitors. She might have her nose holding her back; I had my "very high" standards swatting them off.

#

Dear Diary,

Today, I really was not in the mood. I'm barely awake to write this. I tried cancelling the meeting but auntie said he is already on the way. (Besides the fam, only auntie knows about these meet ups. If word got out that I was seeing suitors, so much negative discussions will come up for seeing so many right after each other).

So I didn't get dressed up. I wore the basic jeans and shirt outfit. My mom raised her brow at the sight but didn't comment.

He turned out to be a neat guy. But he admitted he was only doing this to get his mother off his back. So we just chatted freely without any pretentions about taking this further. If he was a woman I wouldn't have minded trading my phone number with him to keep talking afterwards.

#

Dear Diary,

I cannot.

He asked if I'd take off my hijab after we got married.

I asked him was he intending on taking off his pants in public when we do get married?

Why was he coming to see me if he wanted an unveiled prospective?

#

Dear Diary,

Flowers are nice. Pretty to look at. A bouquet waiting for me at home is nice.

The living room filled from top to bottom with flower bouquets before the guy even arrives to see me is a bit overkill.

It did not help that when they brought in the last bouquet, after keeping it outside for an hour, there were bees hidden in it. We had to keep catching them and releasing them outside. Eight bees, Bader counted.

I can still hear the buzzing of the bees when I'm sitting in my room.

#

Dear Diary,

My cousin asks why I don't just find someone at work? Yes, sure, with all my colleagues are women and the guys who come in are either married, or older than me by twenty years. Sure, that sounds possible. The whole transition of "don't talk to guys" when I was in school, to "don't be friendly with the men at work", to end up at an age where they ask why are there no guys talking to you.

#

Dear Diary,

The guy just kept talking like he's Gaston. One sleazy comment after the other. I just kept looking on as he kept probably parroting all his favorite lines from *Two and a Half Men*. Right in front of my mom and the auntie. His mom probably doesn't understand English, but my mom does. She calmly got up, collected my glass of water, walked over to him, and poured it over his head.

"Make sure he washes his mouth with soap before you let him talk again." My mom told the auntie.

#

Dear Diary,

This one I had to play it safe. He is my friend's brother. I've never met him, even when I hang out at her place. She told me he saw my picture in one of her posts, and wanted to see if I'd like to meet. I promised to give him a chance, but my friend just laughed and said not to stress myself out. Still, I didn't want to cause any weird tension between us, so I tried to be on my best.

He was nice. He shared stories of him and my friend. He talked about studying in the States. I just couldn't see myself with him, in our own apartment, or going out for lunch or the movies. I said yes to meeting again, but I was worried about how to pull it off one more time.

My parents were excited that I said yes for a second meeting. Was I stressing them with this? Were they putting all their hopes on this one? Bader's only comment is that the man supported Barcelona which he did not approve of.

#

Dear Diary,

Today's suitor started name dropping as though he was calling out some kind of attendance sheet. He kept mentioning how he knew this lady, how he knew my uncle, how he knew the prime minister, how he knew the woman behind the megastore, etc. Basically his circle of friends are all the influential people in town.

I asked him if he knew Bu Hamza. He paused, and started saying how yes, he met him once or twice. I nodded and kept gushing over Bu Hamza, hoping he could get us to meet next time. He promised he would, even said he'll text him now, and left.

"Who is Bu Hamza?" My mom, the eavesdropper, asked me once the door closed.

"I don't know, but apparently he knows." I tried not to smile, and my mom as well, even while she was lecturing me for making stories for that "poor boy".

#

Dear Diary,

I skipped on breakfast, since I was late on this meeting. So probably because of my sleepy state, or that I didn't have breakfast, that I misheard the guy. I asked he can repeat again.

His comment was, "Have you thought about joining a gym?"

Now, I know he doesn't work at a gym, so I'm sure he didn't mean to discuss his work. I replied in my sweetest voice that my weight or shape has nothing to do with him, and *3aib* that he even comments on my figure. I didn't wait for him to leave as I exited the living room, not caring how disrespectful it looked. I ignored any attempt from his family for us to meet again.

I didn't want to see others after that. For all my quips and teasings, comments about my weight always get me. Even my brothers don't tease me with that.

#

Dear Diary,

A lady called my mom asking for my photo. Now, this isn't some yearbook request. It's known fact that sometimes they'll ask for a girl's photo, to show to prospective suitors to see if they'll be interested. My parents blanked out when I asked how come we can't do the same in reverse, have the girls collect the boy's photos to see. "the boy *yikhtab*, not the girl" my mom would say.

My mom promised she won't give my photo. She believes our family is known well enough to need to use those steps to attract suitors. I still wonder if there is some book out there with a low quality photo of my Instagram profile picture taped in it. It would read "25, working, single" probably, with "Warning: three brothers"

#

Dear Diary,

Today a guy chased me in the car all the way to home. I've been chased once or twice, on the Gulf Road, but never all the way to home. I keep thinking to outrun him, but I keep remembering my dad's words, that no matter what, to just drive slow and drive home. It's fine if he finds our house, just come home.

I made a dash for the indoor parking. My car is usually parked outside, but I didn't feel safe, knowing his car is parked right behind me. The driver comes out to see what is going on, and I felt worried for him. I didn't want him to get in trouble or be beaten by this random dude. Thankfully, he only honked and drove away, laughing with his car windows rolled down. Asshole.

I hope his tire flattens while he's driving, let him feel the fear of not being in control of his driving. And wondering if he was ever one of the suitors who came to see me.

#

Dear Diary,

Bader kept saying no to every suitor who called this week. Or technically, the aunts of the suitor. I don't think the guys even knew their aunts were calling for them. Still, Bader was in a mood, and being the eldest, thought he had a say in who comes to see me. My mom and I gave each other a look as Bader kept talking with my dad. Just to spite him, I said yes to everyone who called to meet. I didn't need him to get the idea that he can actually control my own future.

#

Dear Diary,

I don't recall what this suitor did for a living, but it's not like I had a chance. We were just getting to chat when Salman came to say hello to my mom and recognized the guy. They went to the same university. Instead of just saying hello and leaving, Salman actually came and sat next to him and they started to discuss. The guy seemed distracted about balancing attention between me and my brother, but once my brother brought up a name, they both completely forgot about me and started to catch up. I just caught up on my messages while they chatted.

#

Dear Diary,

He huffed. He literally huffed, as though I was boring him. I didn't even say anything! His knee kept tapping against the couch, and he had the audacity to look at his watch once. I asked if he had an appointment, and he said no, and leaned back in his seat. Not another word but a sigh every few moment. I tried to cajole him into talking, but he seemed unbothered by the whole thing. I was close to asking him to blink twice if he was abducted and brought here. As soon as the appropriate twenty minutes passed, he straightens up, thanked me for my time and left.

I kept asking my parents if they had paid someone to bring him over. Still no idea to this day what his deal was.

#

Dear Diary,

You were nearly found by Salman. He came in looking for something, and you, silly thing, was out on my desk. Hopefully he didn't get to read much. Hell, I feel awkward to reread anything on here.

#

Dear Diary,

I met again with Ahmad (my friend's brother, not my brother). Ahmad came this time alone, with the auntie. My mom still stayed nearby, chatting on the phone with my uncle. I can hear her voice carry over to where we are sitting, glancing and smiling at each other. This time he started the conversation, asked about my interest and hobbies. I kept speaking a mix of English and Arabic, while he kept talking in Kuwaiti. I wasn't sure he caught on what I was saying, but seeing that he studied in the states, I assumed he understood English. We had different taste in music, but we did watch some of the same Kuwaiti soap opera (he liked them, I mocked them). I sensed he had other questions, but we went at slow pace, talking about general stuff. He finally asked about whether I wanted kids. I told him yes, but not as soon as I got married, maybe later on. He admitted he wants kids as well, and won't mind waiting.

He asked if he can see me again. I said yes (there was no real reason to say no).

Was I attracted to him? No. was it easy to talk to him? Yes. Does there need to be attraction to look seriously into marrying someone? I don't know. I know Disney isn't realistic, and seeing as nothing went wrong, why not see if this can develop further?

My friend texted me afterwards that he was excited and telling her parents about the meetup. I smiled at the text, and hoped this was for the best.

CPSIA information can be obtained
at www.ICGtesting.com
Printed in the USA
BVHW052002060623
665497BV00015B/944